Other Books by Mitsumasa Anno
Published by Philomel Books:

Anno's Animals
Anno's Britain
Anno's Counting House
Anno's Italy
Anno's Journey
Anno's Magical ABC:
  An Anamorphic Alphabet
Anno's Medieval World
Anno's Mysterious Multiplying Jar
The King's Flower
The Unique World of Mitsumasa Anno:
  Selected Works (1968–1977)

First U.S.A. edition 1983
Published by Philomel Books, a division of
The Putnam Publishing Group, 51 Madison Avenue, New York NY 10010.
Originally Published in 1983 by Fukuinkan Shoten Publishers, Tokyo
as *Tabi No Ehon IV* by Mitsumasa Anno, copyright © 1983 by Kuso-kobo.
All rights reserved. Printed in Japan.

Library of Congress Cataloging in Publication Data
Anno, Mitsumasa, Anno's U.S.A.
    Translation of: Tabi no ehon, IV.
    Summary: In wordless panoramas a lone traveler
approaches the New World from the West in the present
day and journeys the width of the country backward
through time, departing the east coast as the Santa
Maria appears over the horizon.
    [1. United States—Pictorial works. 2. Stories
without words] I. Title.
PZ7.A5875As 1983 [Fic] 83-13107
ISBN 0-399-20974-3
ISBN 0-399-21060-1 paperback

Afterword

As a child in Tsuwano, a small town in western Japan, Mitsumasa Anno felt an intense curiosity about the ocean that lay beyond the mountains surrounding the green and beautiful valley in which he lived. When, at the age of ten, he finally made the journey to the ocean, he immediately began to wonder about the countries across the sea.

In 1963 he made his first visit to Europe, a visit that resulted ultimately in his book *Anno's Journey*. Since then, with sketchbook and camera in hand, he has made several more trips to Europe and the British isles, recording his observations in *Anno's Italy* and *Anno's Britain*. A brief trip to the United States in 1977 opened his eyes to the wonders of the New World, and he returned in the autumn of 1981 for a longer stay.

Already familiar with America's art, literature and history, as well as its famous children's books, its films and folklore, Mr. Anno arrived with some idea of what he wanted to see, and a preconceived notion of how he would proceed. As he had done in Europe and in Britain, he planned to rent a car and simply drive at leisure from one end of the country to the other, inviting serendipitous views, events and insights. But the immense scale of America's geography came as a shock, as it often does to newcomers to its shores. Nevertheless, he managed to cover an astonishing amount of territory according to his original plan, exploring bustling cities and quiet country byways at his own pace, savoring the special qualities of each part of the United States and its richly mixed population.

As always in his journeying, he preferred the woods and green fields, the mountains and fertile farmlands, but he also visited the cities with their striking architecture and their busy inhabitants. Only Anno could find a way to show modern New York City without cars! The city's streets are filled, not